Look for Trucks!

By Gina Ingoglia
Illustrated by Tom LaPadula

A GOLDEN BOOK • NEW YORK
Western Publishing Company, Inc., Racine, Wisconsin 53404

The moving van was packed and ready to go.

"Please take care of my bike," said Charlie. "It's brand-new!"

"Don't worry!" said the driver. "We'll take it straight to your new house!"

Charlie and his family got into their car.

"I hope we see the van on the road," said Charlie. "Then I'll know my bike is safe."

"Look for all kinds of trucks," said his father. "Then you won't have time to worry."

"I see one now!" said Charlie. A sanitation truck was across the street.

They drove through town. A delivery truck was dropping off fresh fruit and vegetables at the grocery store. A mail truck had stopped to pick up letters for the post office.

Lots of trucks were on the highway. A transport truck roared by. It was carrying six new pickup trucks.

"There's a horse van," said Charlie. "Now all I have to find is a *moving van*!"

The air got very dusty. A road construction crew was working hard.

A front-end loader loaded gravel into a waiting dump truck. A concrete mixer mixed fresh concrete in a big metal drum. A spreader smoothed out the rough ground.

"Look at the huge wheels on that truck," said Charlie.

"It's called an off-road dump truck," said his mother. "It can carry extra-heavy loads."

"It looks like it could carry *everything*!" said Charlie.

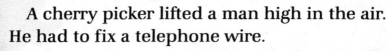

A cherry picker lifted a man high in the air. He had to fix a telephone wire.

"There goes a tow truck," said Charlie. "It's pulling a broken-down car. I hope our moving van doesn't break down!"

A motor home passed them. It had green curtains in the windows.

"Look at that!" said Charlie. "Those people take their house around with them."

Charlie looked out the back window.
"Wow!" he said. "Here comes an eighteen-
wheeler!" Charlie waved to the driver.

FIRE DEPARTMENT

Charlie's father turned off the highway.
Nearby, a bell clanged loudly.
  "There's a firehouse!" shouted Charlie.
"The engines are coming out!"

A hook and ladder truck and a pumper raced into the street. In a few seconds the trucks were gone.

They drove down a shady street. Charlie spotted a parked ice-cream truck.

"There's a truck I'd like to get a good close look at!" he said.

Charlie's father laughed. "What luck!" he said. "We were going to stop anyway. Look ahead and you'll see why!"

"There's our moving van!" shouted Charlie. "We're here!"

And standing right next to it was Charlie's brand-new bike.